BASEBALL

Foreword by Phil Patton

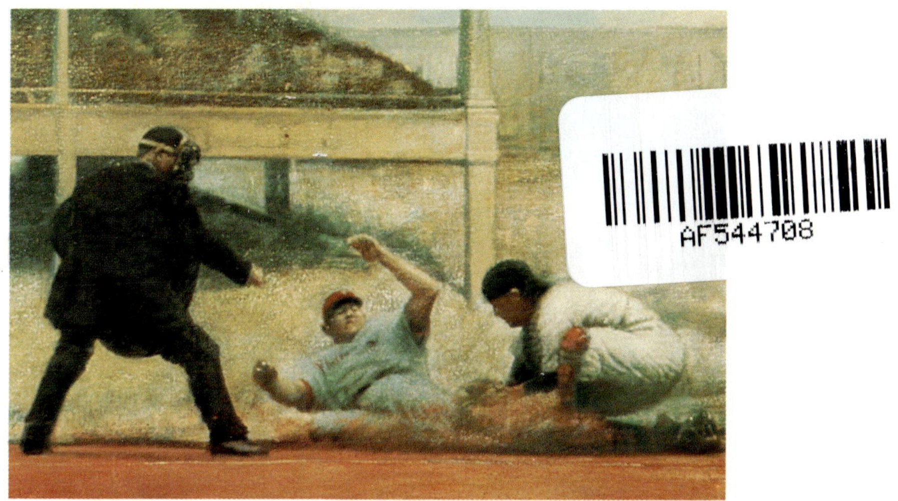

FAWCETT COLUMBINE · NEW YORK

A Fawcett Columbine Book
Published by Ballantine Books

ISBN: 0-449-90487-3

Cover design by Richard Aquan
Cover art: John Dobbs, *Play at Third*
(oil on linen, 1982, 36″ x 40″).
Courtesy of the artist.
Manufactured in the United States of America

First Edition: April 1990

10 9 8 7 6 5 4 3 2

FOREWORD

Baseball is a subject so full of powerful icons and dramatic poses that it possesses an irresistable lure for the artist. A dance of essential moments arrayed on a geometric landscape, baseball is itself art.

Thomas Eakins, also famous for his views of rowers and wrestlers, became one of the first painters of the game. Artists of all styles, from popular to pop, followed. While Norman Rockwell turned baseball scenes into vignettes of middle-American, mid-century life, Claes Oldenburg transformed the equipment of the game into pop icons in his monumental mitts and bats. Jeffrey Rubin paints over photographs of baseball players in action, redeeming the mass media clichés.

The game is also, of course, a game of stars. A batter's style—as Harvey Dinnerstein's "The Wide Swing," a portrait of Joe Dimaggio at the plate, shows—is as much his signature as the one he pens on souvenir balls. Style is the way the player makes baseball his own—and the way the artist does too.

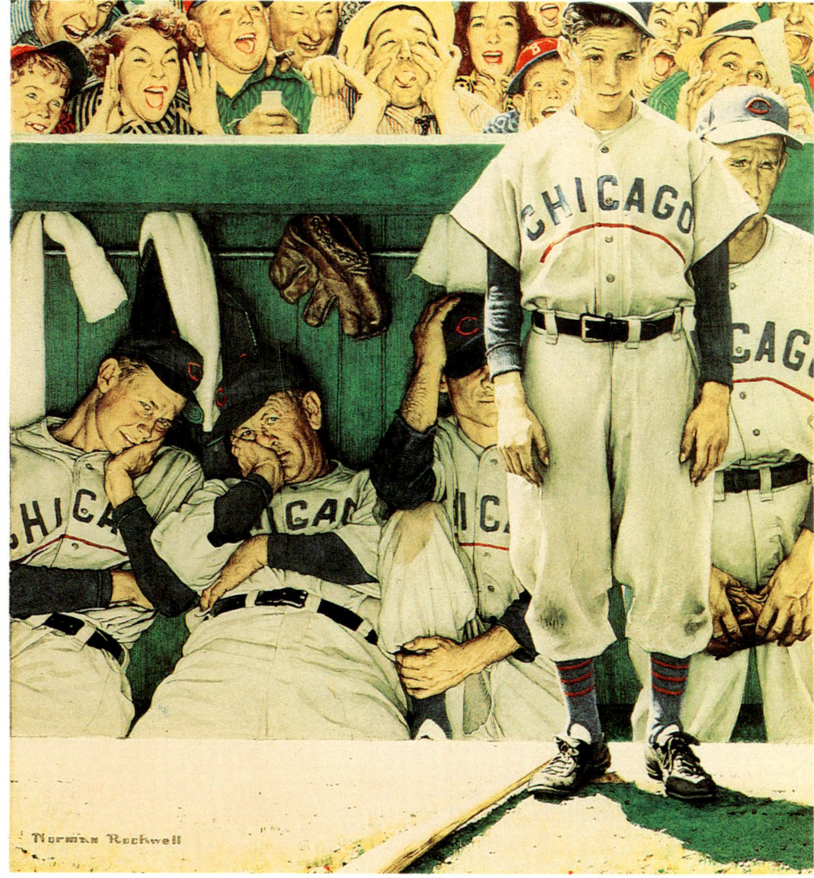
CHICAGO
Norman Rockwell

NORMAN ROCKWELL

The Dugout (1948)

COURTESY OF THE NORMAN ROCKWELL MUSEUM AT STOCKBRIDGE, STOCKBRIDGE, MA, PRINTED BY PERMISSION OF THE ESTATE OF NORMAN ROCKWELL,

FAWCETT COLUMBINE • NEW YORK

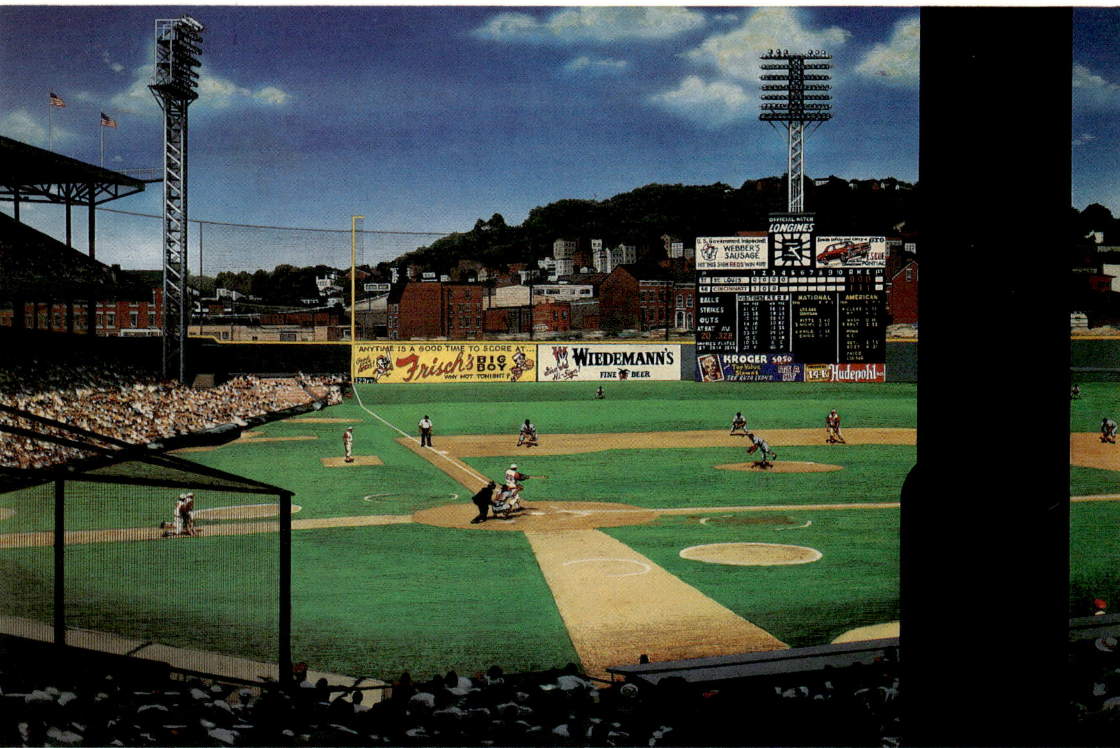
OFFICIAL WATCH
LONGINES
U.S. Government Inspected!
WEBBER'S SAUSAGE
HIT THIS SIGN REDS WIN 4100
BALLS
STRIKES
OUTS
AT BAT AV.
20 .328
ST. LOUIS
CINCINNATI
NATIONAL
AMERICAN
"ANYTIME IS A GOOD TIME TO SCORE AT...
Frisch's BIG BOY
WHY NOT TONIGHT?
WIEDEMANN'S
FINE BEER
KROGER
Top Value Stamps
SEE RUTH LYONS
ITS A HIT
14-K Hudepohl

BILL PURDOM
Crosley Field Revisited (1989)
Offset lithograph, edition/600, 21⅝″ x 29⅝″
PUBLISHED BY BILL GOFF, INC.,
PO BOX 508 GRACIE STATION, NEW YORK, NY 10028

FAWCETT COLUMBINE • NEW YORK

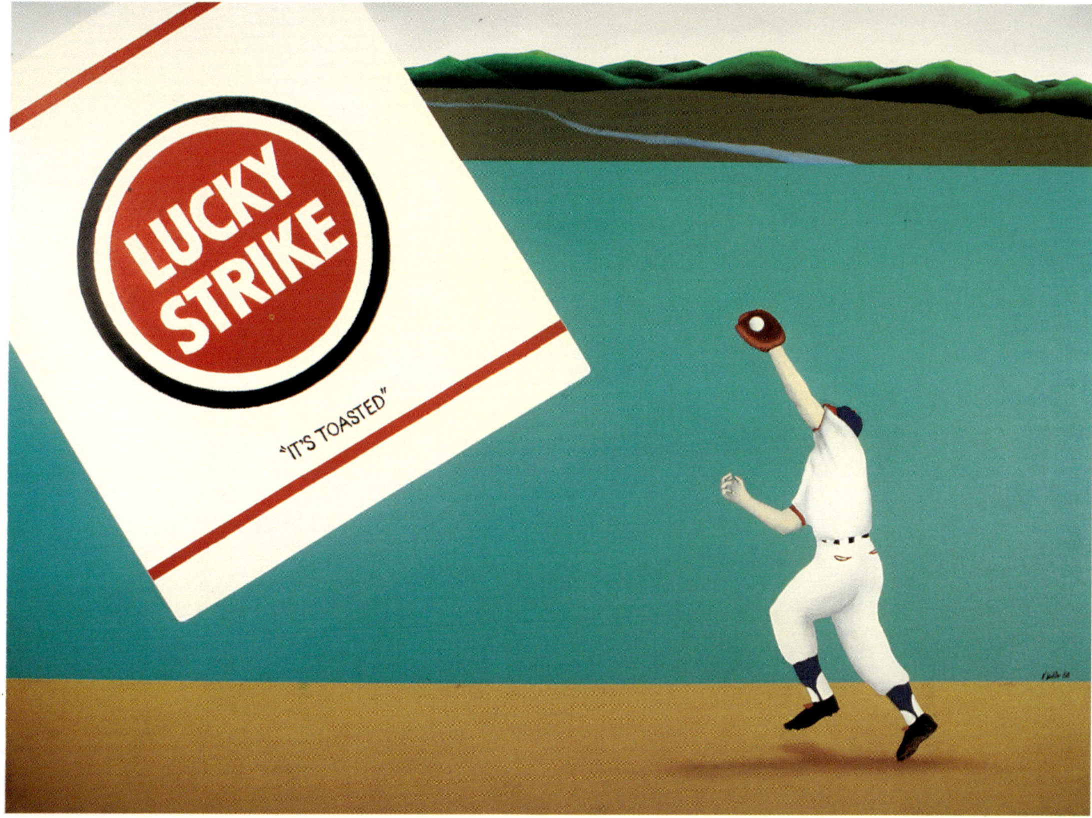
LUCKY
STRIKE
"IT'S TOASTED"

VINCENT SCILLA
Baseball in Big Sky Country (Lucky Strike) (1988)
Oil on canvas, 24″ x 32″
COLLECTION LAWRENCE WALDMAN

FAWCETT COLUMBINE • NEW YORK

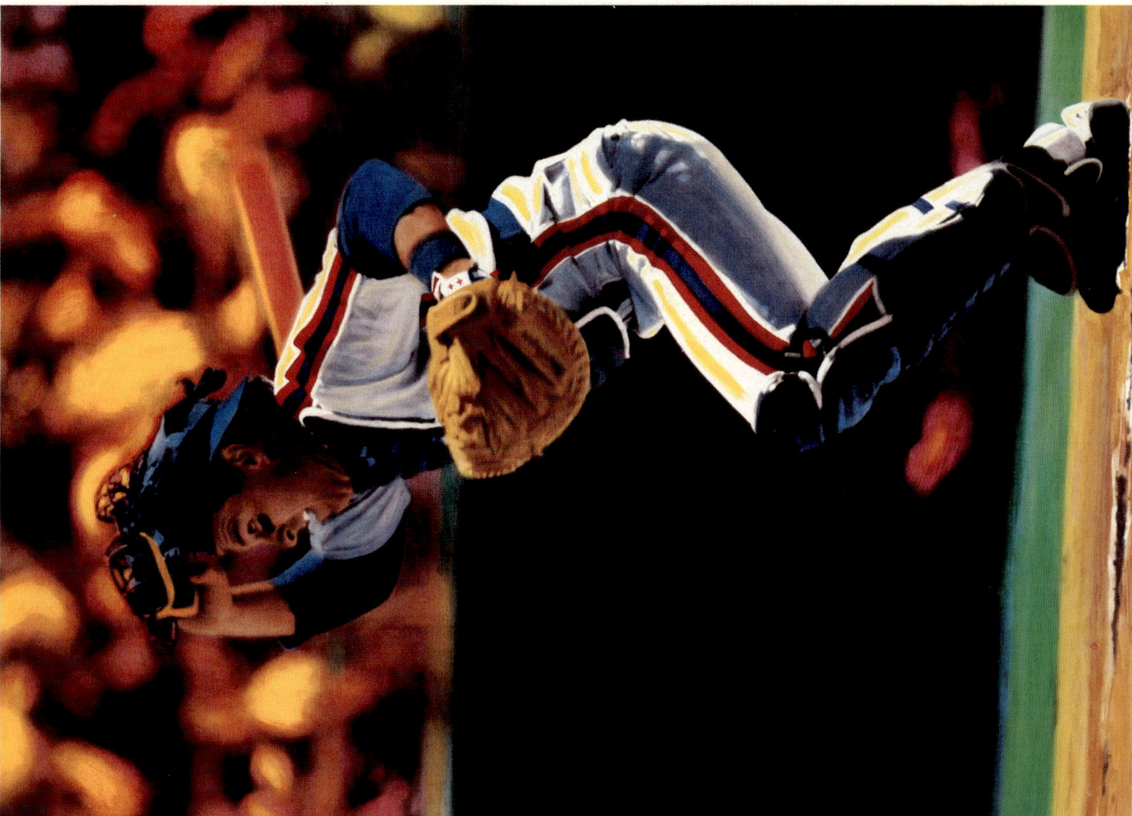

JEFFREY RUBIN
Gary Carter (1989)
Oil on b&w photo, 56″ x 41″

FAWCETT COLUMBINE • NEW YORK

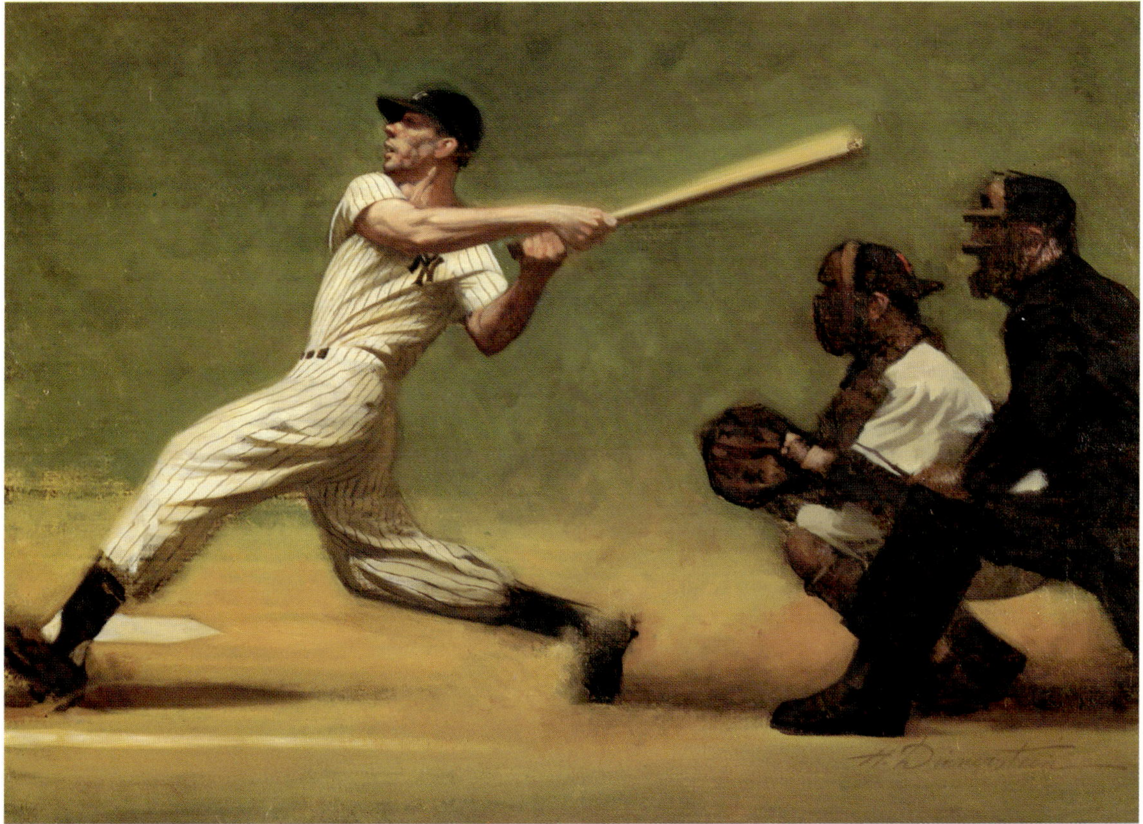

HARVEY DINNERSTEIN
The Wide Swing (1974)
COLLECTION OF CAPRICORN GALLERIES, BETHESDA, MD

FAWCETT COLUMBINE • NEW YORK

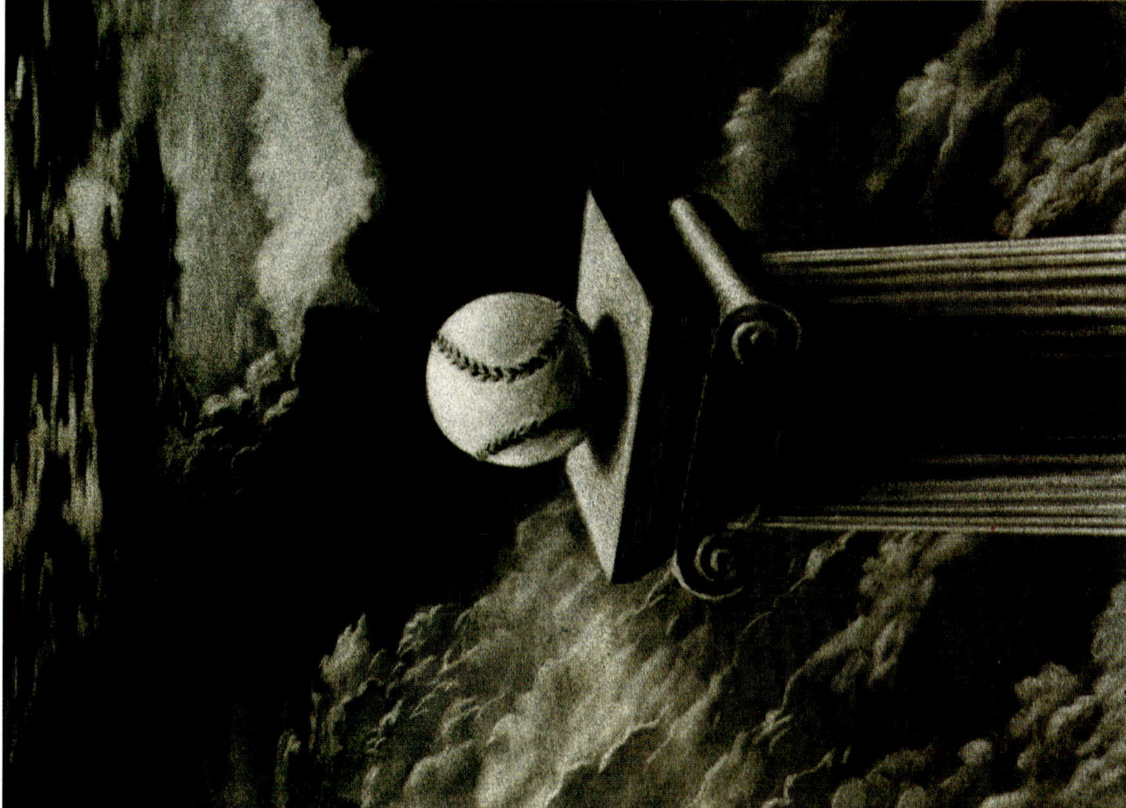

JIM SULLIVAN
Game Ball (1987)
COURTESY OF NANCY HOFFMAN GALLERY , NEW YORK

FAWCETT COLUMBINE • NEW YORK

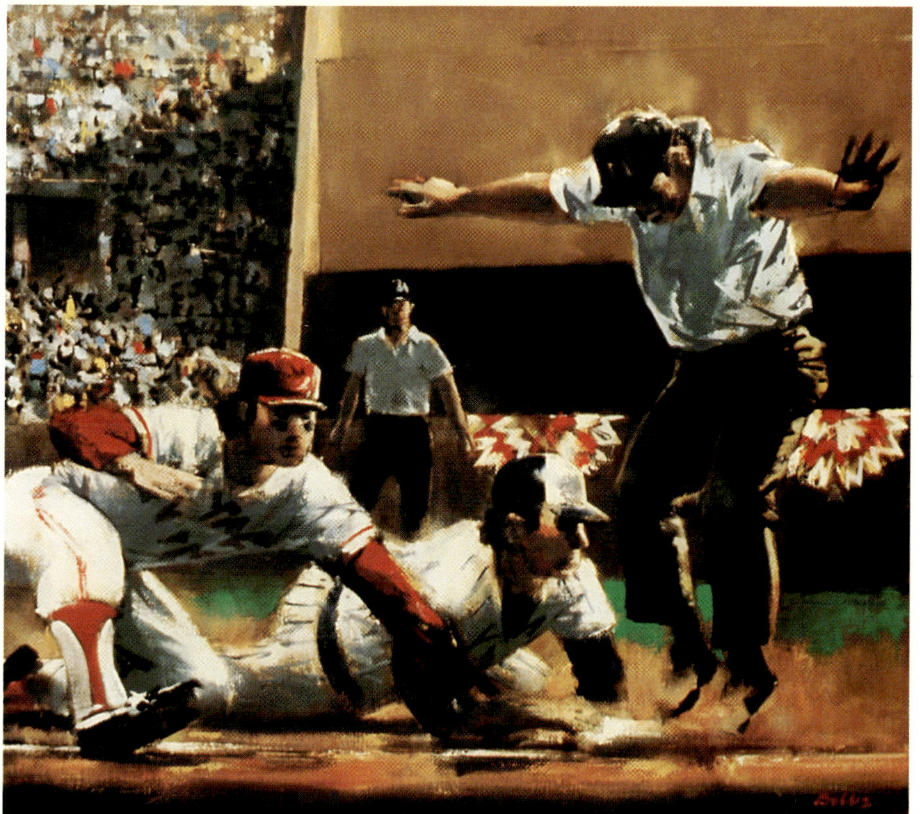

JOHN DOBBS
Play at Third (1982)
Oil on linen, 36″ x 40″
COLLECTION OF THE ARTIST

FAWCETT COLUMBINE • NEW YORK

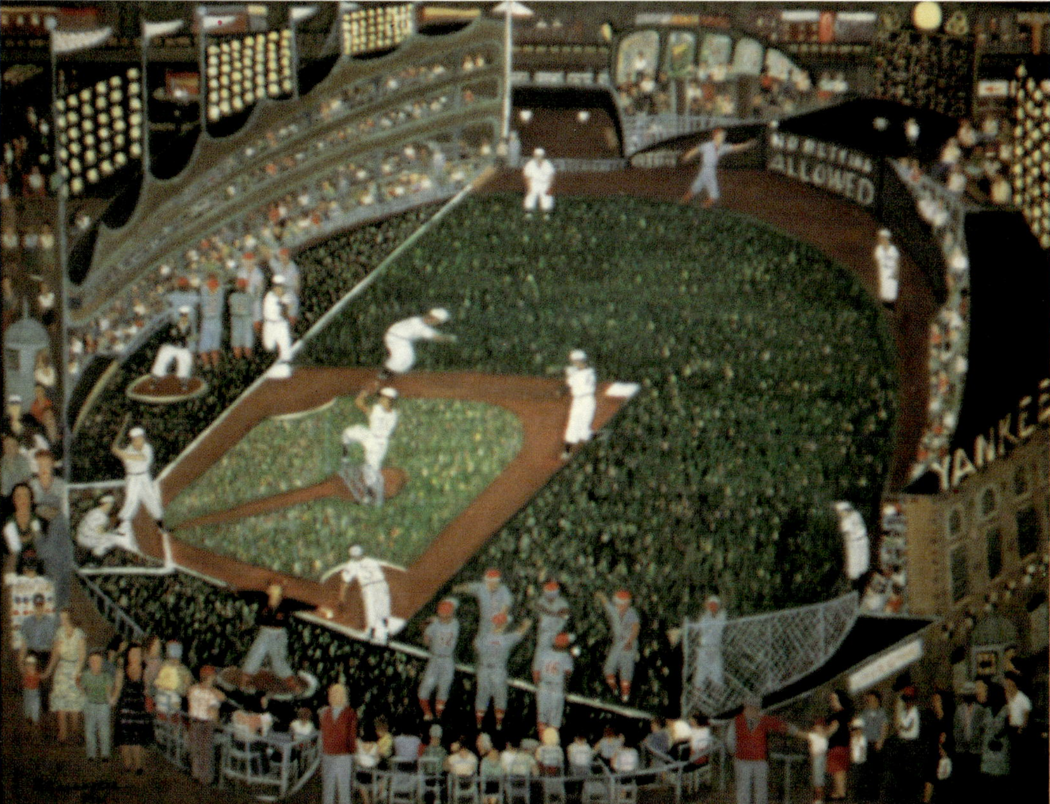
ALLOWED

RALPH FASANELLA
Night Game, Ball Park (1967)
30" x 40"
PRIVATE COLLECTION

FAWCETT COLUMBINE • NEW YORK

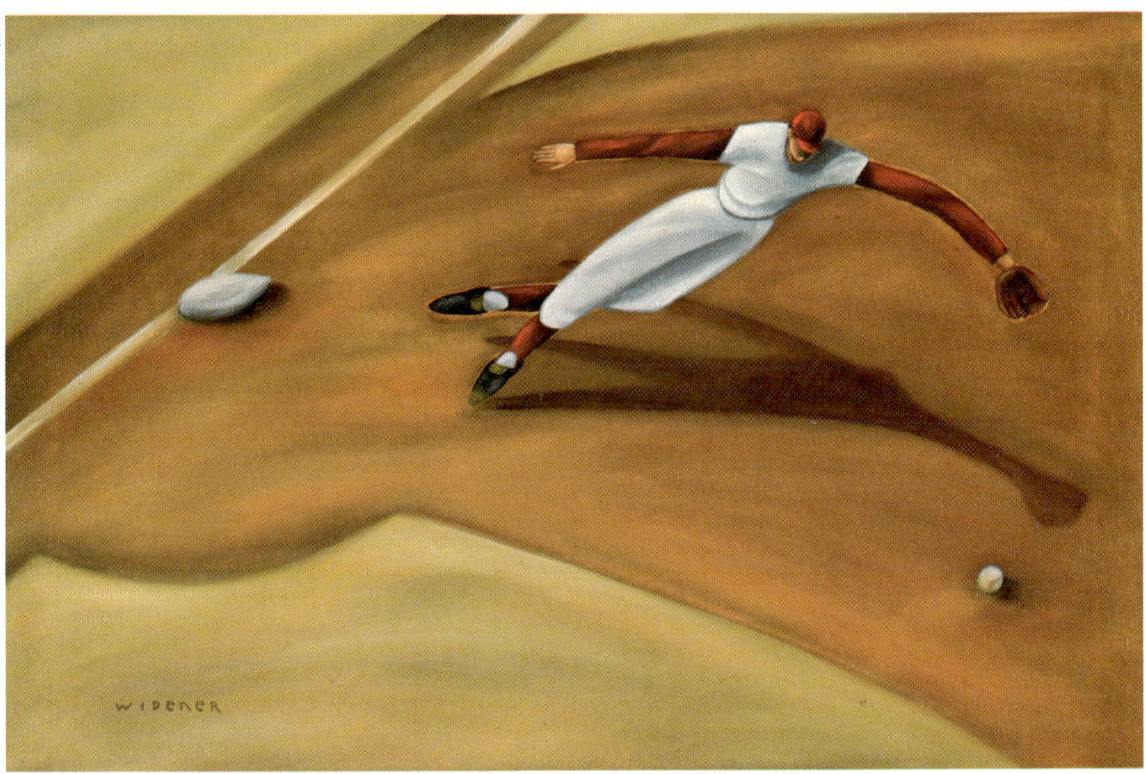
WIDENER

TERRY WIDENER

Untitled (1989)

PRIVATE COLLECTION

FAWCETT COLUMBINE • NEW YORK

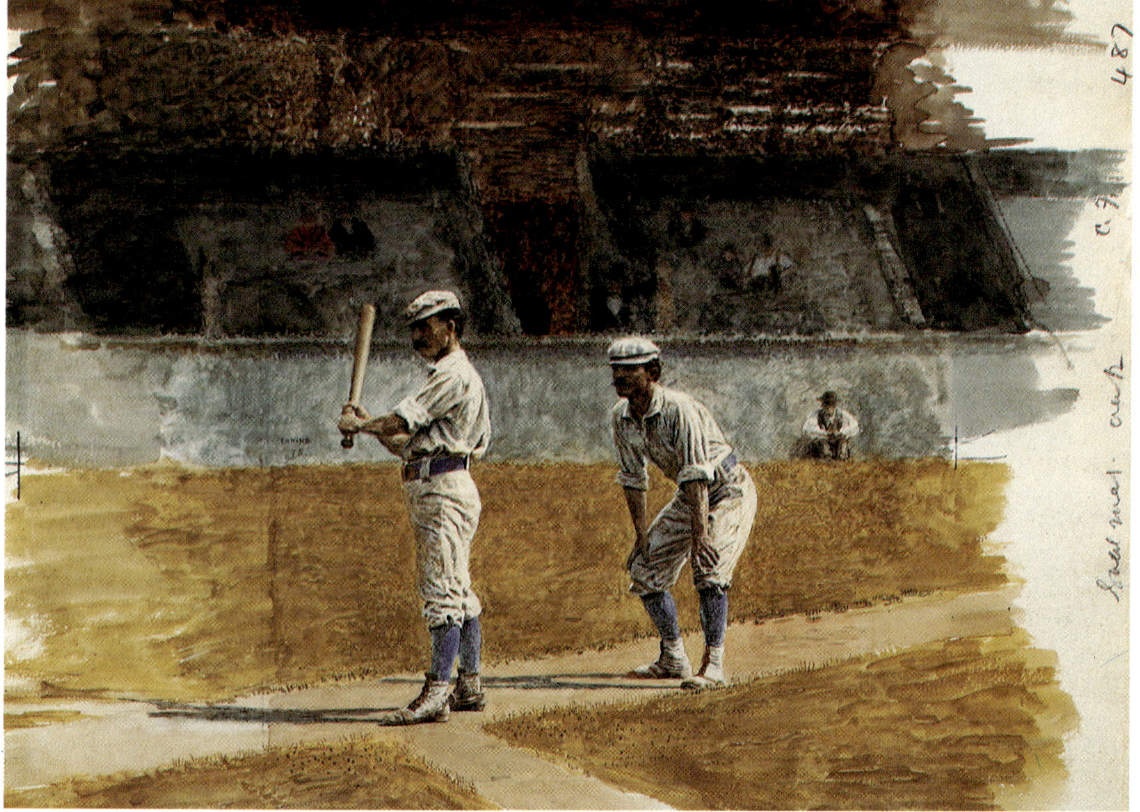

THOMAS EAKINS
Baseball Players Practicing (1875)
Watercolor and pencil on paper
MUSEUM OF ART, RHODE ISLAND SCHOOL OF DESIGN, PROVIDENCE, RHODE ISLAND, JESSE METCALF AND WALTER H. KIMBALL FUNDS

FAWCETT COLUMBINE • NEW YORK

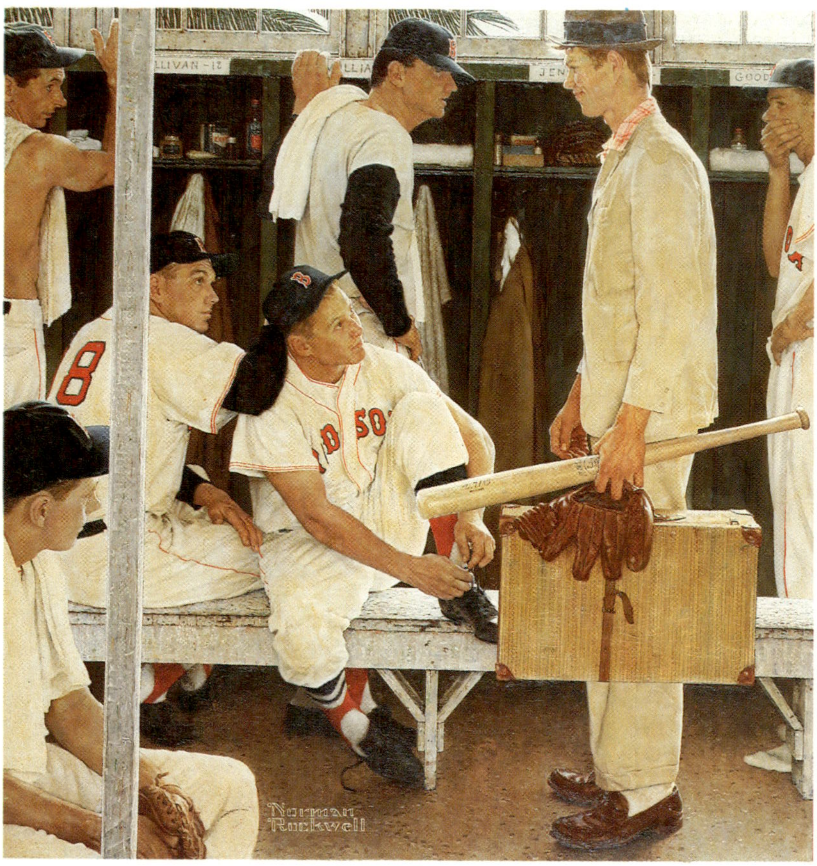
Norman Rockwell

NORMAN ROCKWELL
The Rookie (1957)

FAWCETT COLUMBINE • NEW YORK

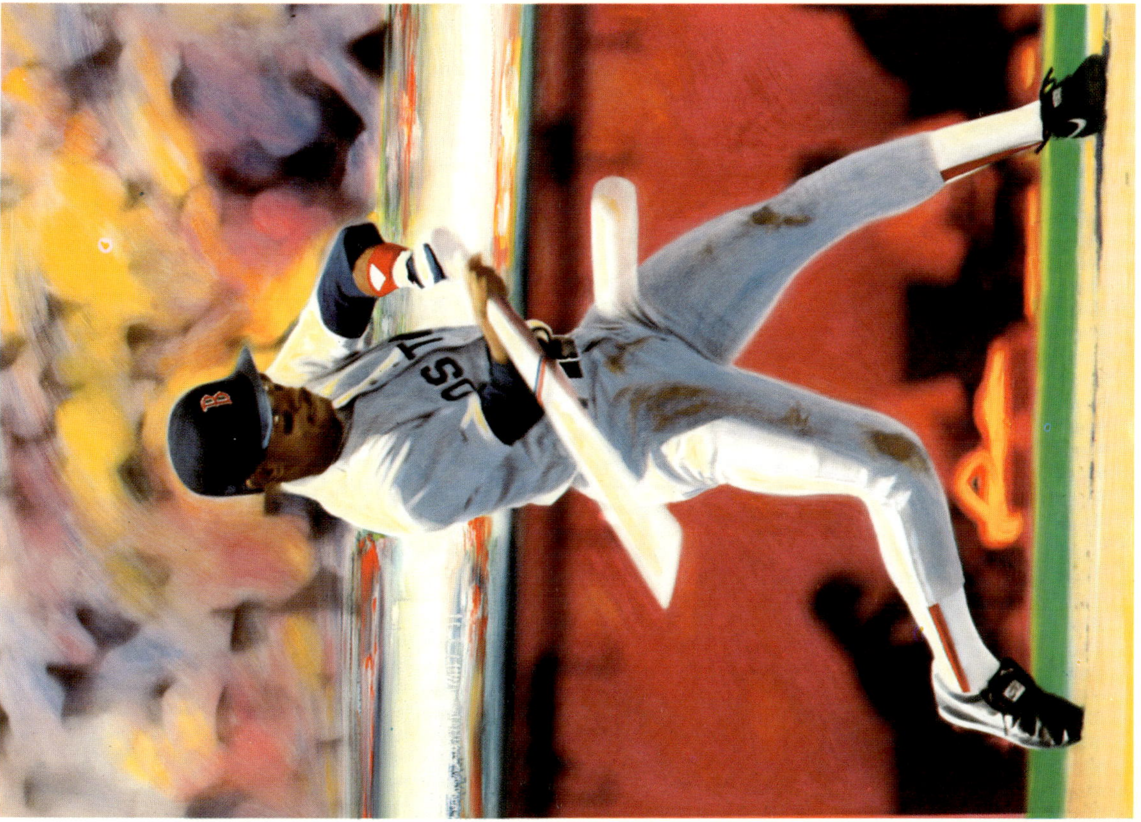

JEFFREY RUBIN
Ellis Burks (1989)
Oil on b&w photo, 56″ x 41″

FAWCETT COLUMBINE • NEW YORK

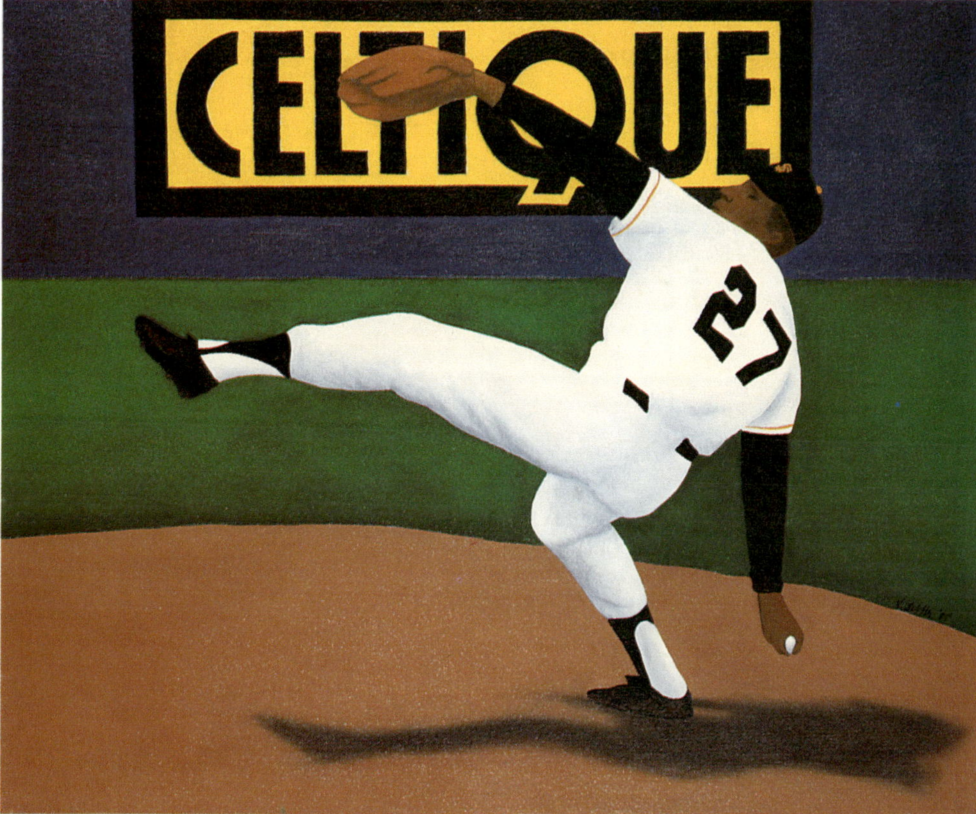
CELTIQUE
27

VINCENT SCILLA
Celtique (1985)
Oil on canvas, 20″ x 24″
COLLECTION KEIICHI SATO

FAWCETT COLUMBINE • NEW YORK

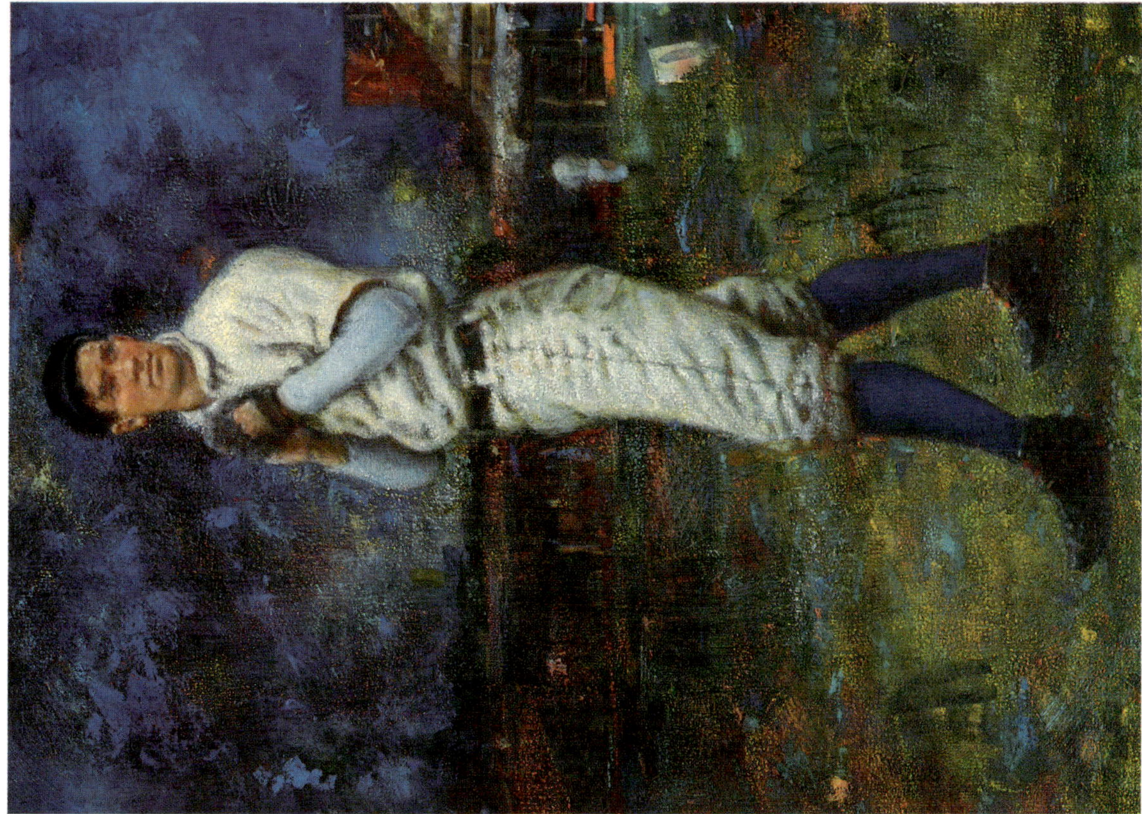

LANCE RICHBOURG
Christy Mathewson (1984)
Oil on canvas, 70″ x 50″
PHOTO CREDIT: D. JAMES DEE
COURTESY O.K. HARRIS GALLERY, NYC.

FAWCETT COLUMBINE • NEW YORK

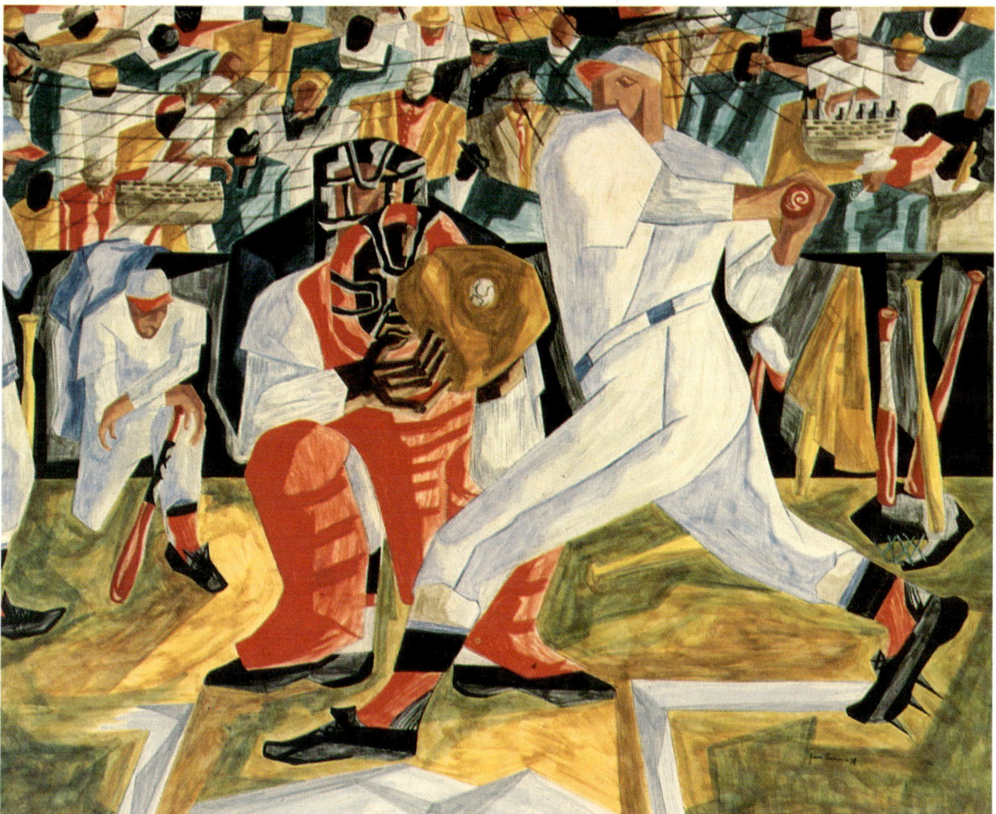

JACOB LAWRENC

Strike (1949)

COLLECTION OF HOWARD UNIVERSITY GALLERY OF ART

FAWCETT COLUMBINE • NEW YORK

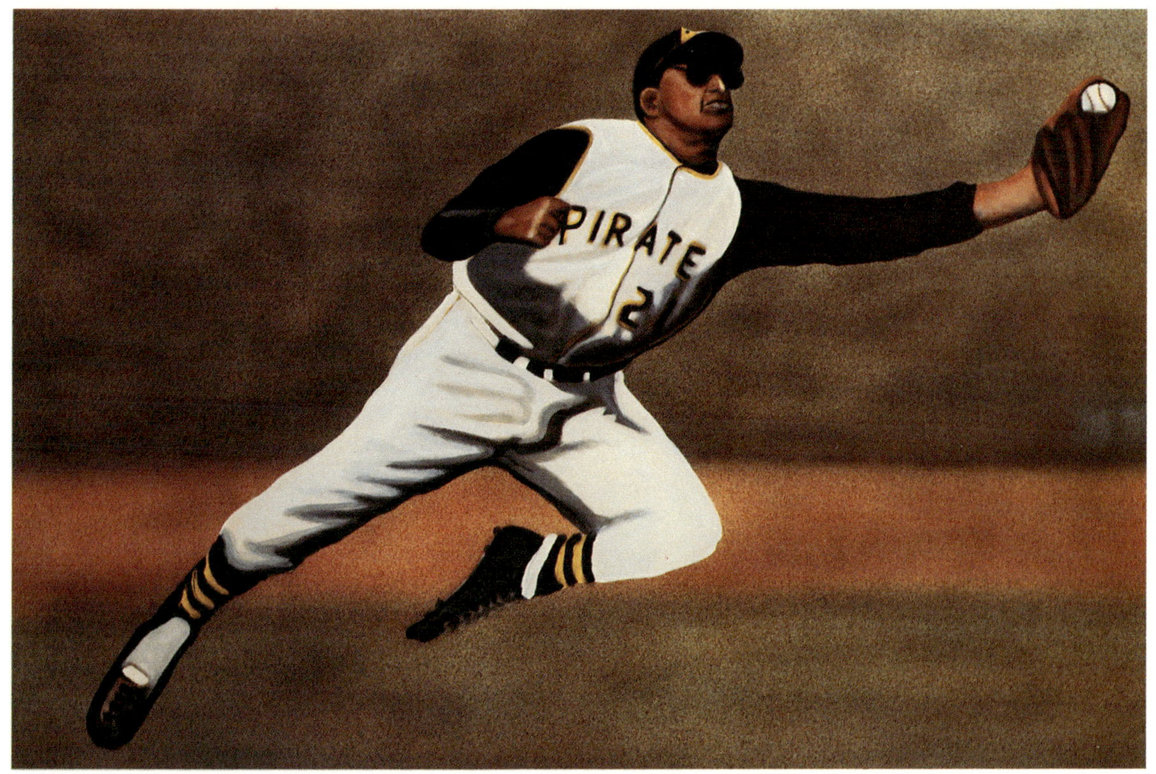
PIRATE
2

RON COHEN
Roberto Clemente (1980)
Acrylic on board, 24″ x 40″
GANZ COLLECTION

FAWCETT COLUMBINE • NEW YORK

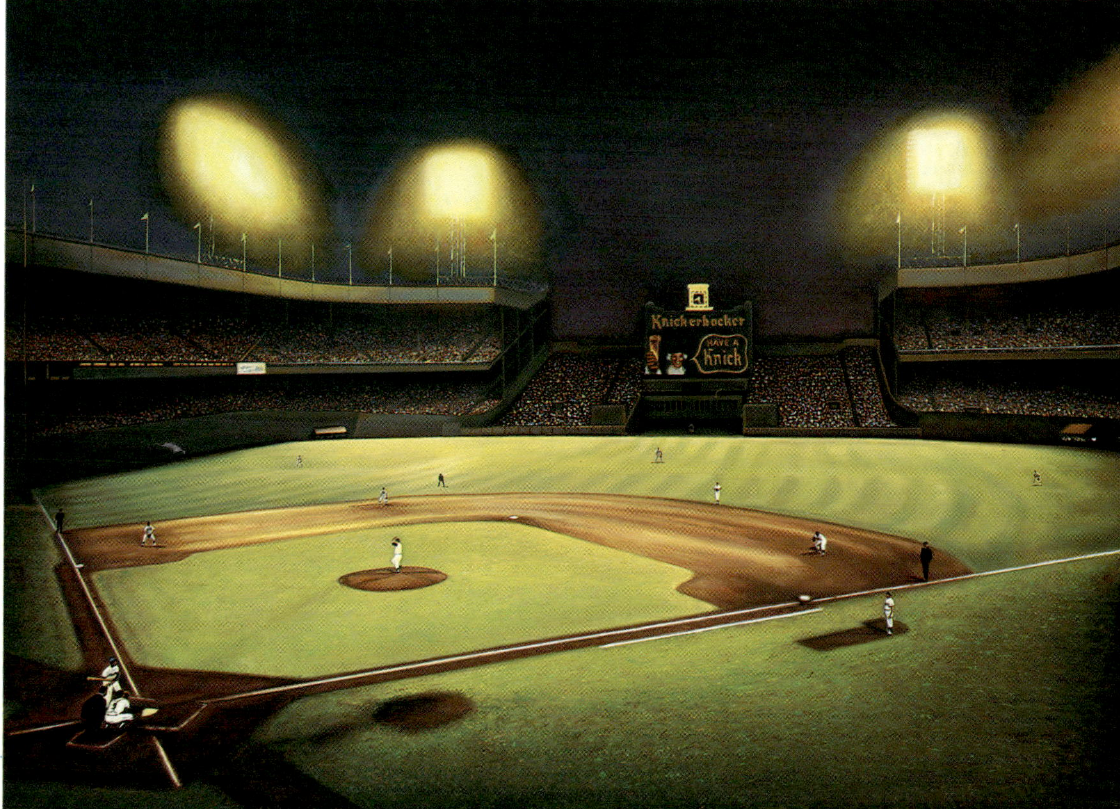
Knickerbocker
HAVE A Knick

WILLIAM FELDMAN
Polo Grounds Nocturne (1988)
Offset lithograph, edition/500, 21⅝" x 29⅝"
PUBLISHED BY BILL GOFF, INC.,
PO BOX 508, GRACIE STATION, NEW YORK, NY 10028

FAWCETT COLUMBINE • NEW YORK

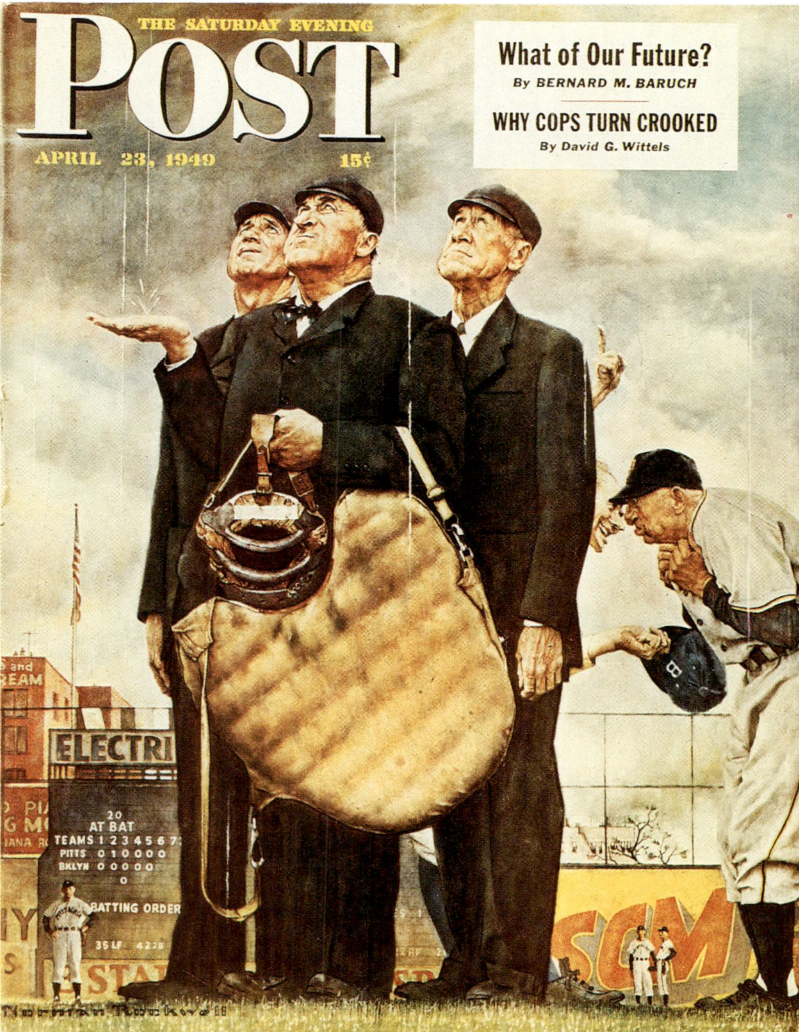
THE SATURDAY EVENING
POST
APRIL 23, 1949
15¢
What of Our Future?
By BERNARD M. BARUCH
WHY COPS TURN CROOKED
By David G. Wittels
ELECTRI
20
AT BAT
TEAMS 1 2 3 4 5 6 7
PITTS 0 1 0 0 0 0
BKLYN 0 0 0 0 0
0
BATTING ORDER
35 LF 422B

NORMAN ROCKWELL

Bottom of the Sixth (Tough Call) (1949)

COURTESY OF THE NORMAN ROCKWELL MUSEUM AT STOCKBRIDGE, STOCKBRIDGE, MA, PRINTED BY PERMISSION OF THE ESTATE OF NORMAN ROCKWELL,

FAWCETT COLUMBINE • NEW YORK

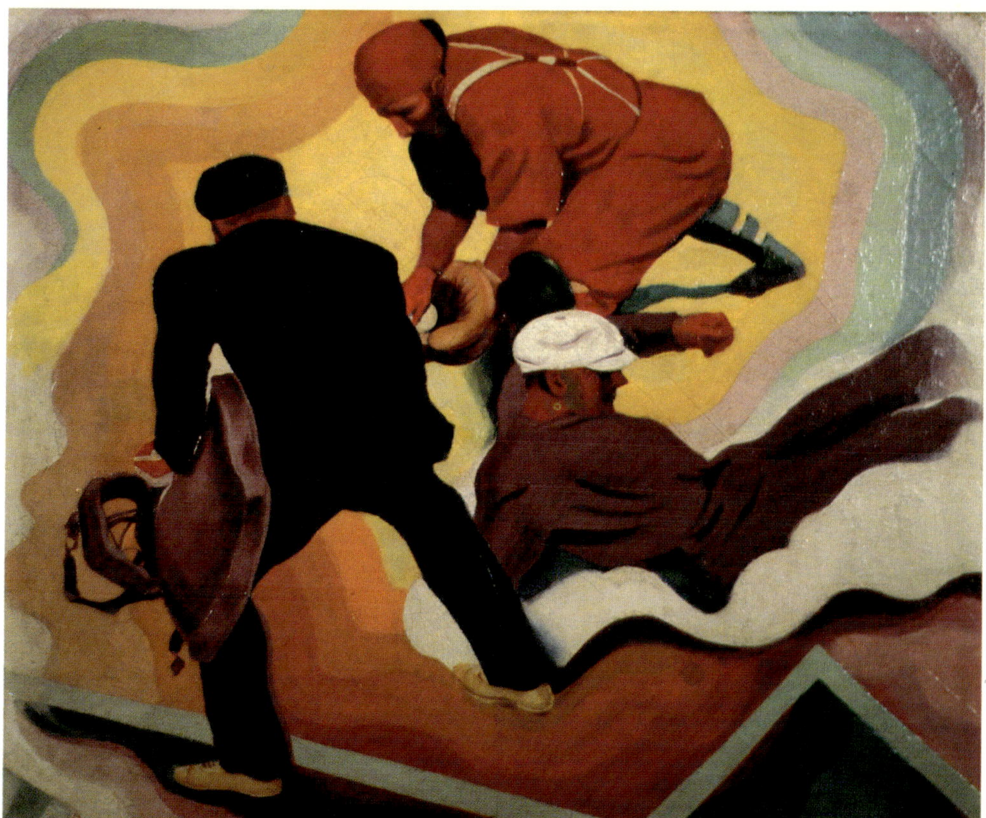

BRAVERMAN
Safe (c. 1936)
COLLECTION OF NEWARK VALLEY CENTRAL SCHOOL DISTRICT,
WPA FEDERAL ART PROJECT

FAWCETT COLUMBINE • NEW YORK

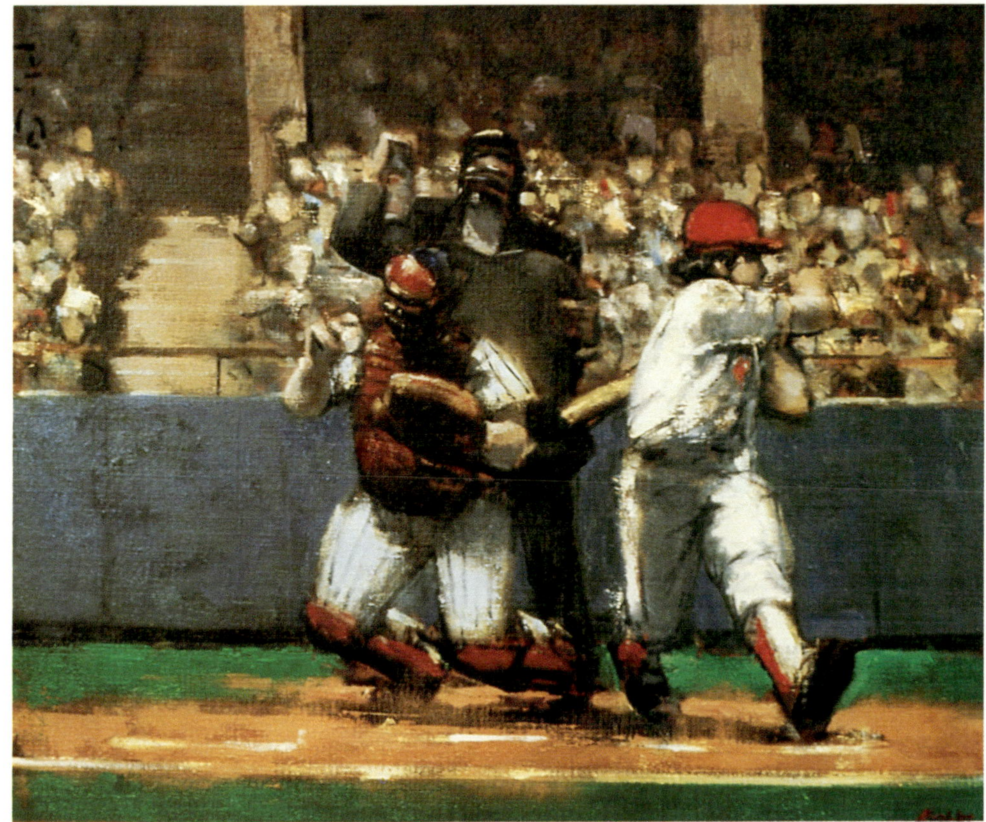

JOHN DOBBS
Going Down Swinging (1982)
Oil on linen, 16″ x 20″
COLLECTION OF ARTIST

FAWCETT COLUMBINE • NEW YORK

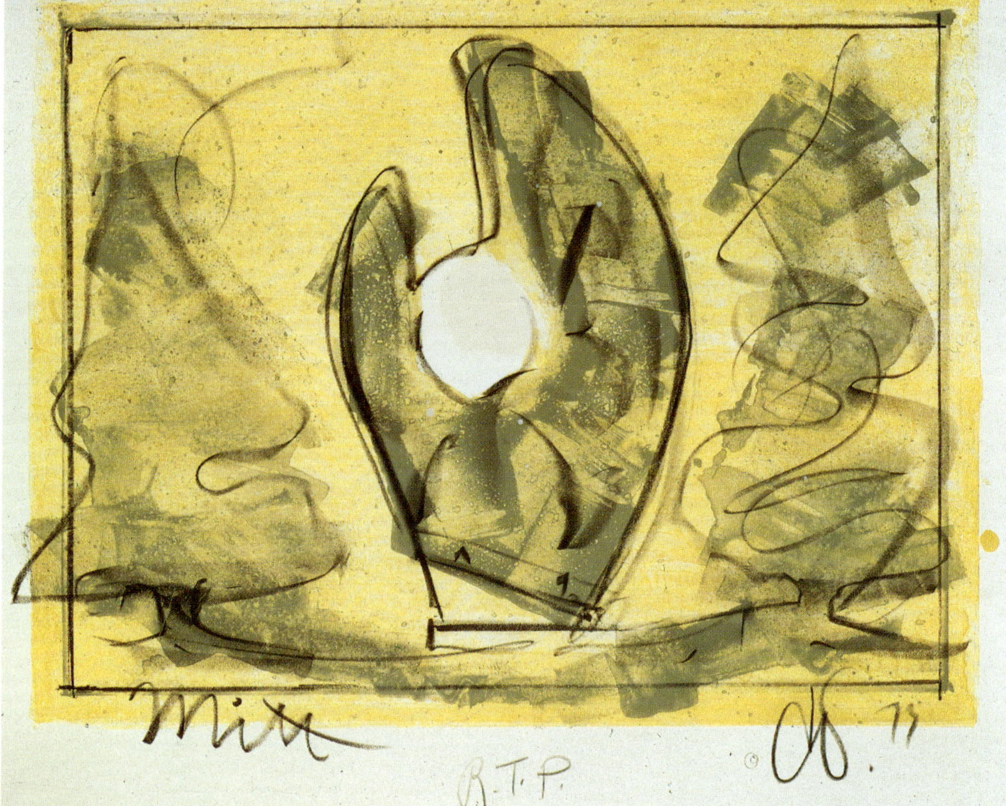
Mill
R.T.P.

CLAES OLDENBURG
Mitt (1973)
COURTESY OF LANDFALL PRESS, INC.

FAWCETT COLUMBINE • NEW YORK

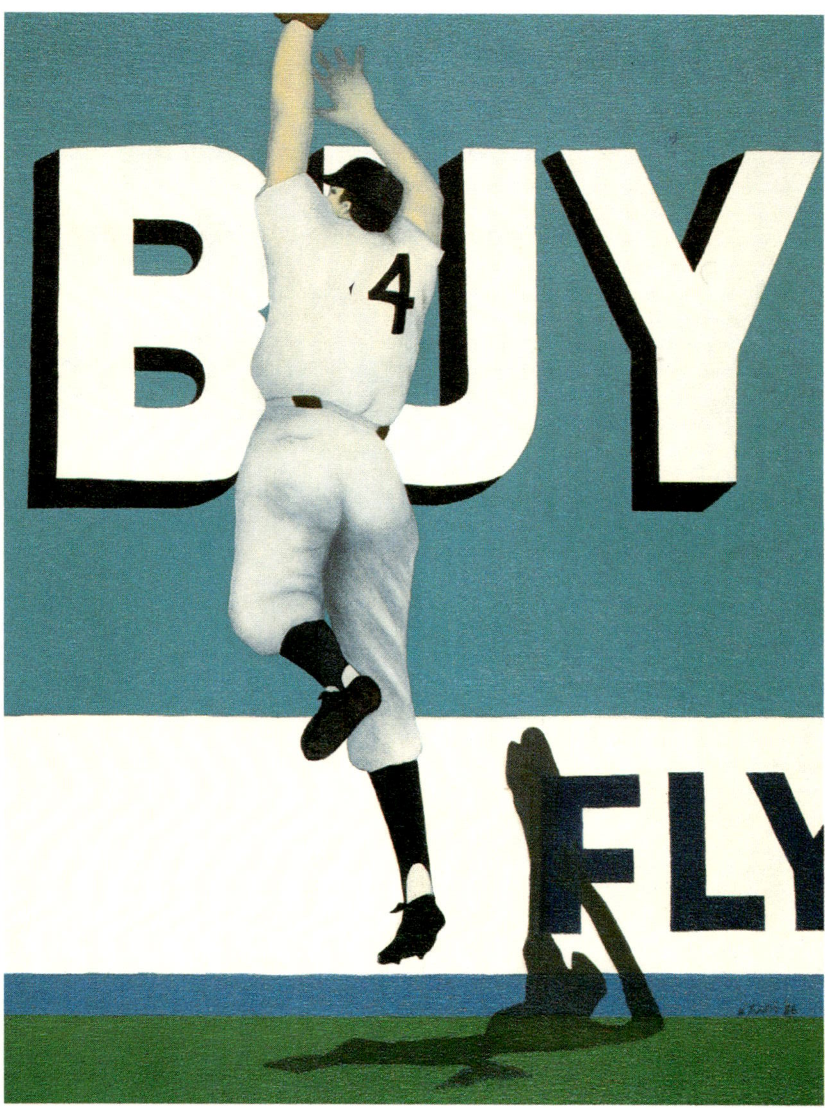
BUY
4
FLY

VINCENT SCILLA
Buy and Fly (1986)
Oil on canvas, 20″ x 26″
COLLECTION JEFFREY FREEDMAN

FAWCETT COLUMBINE • NEW YORK

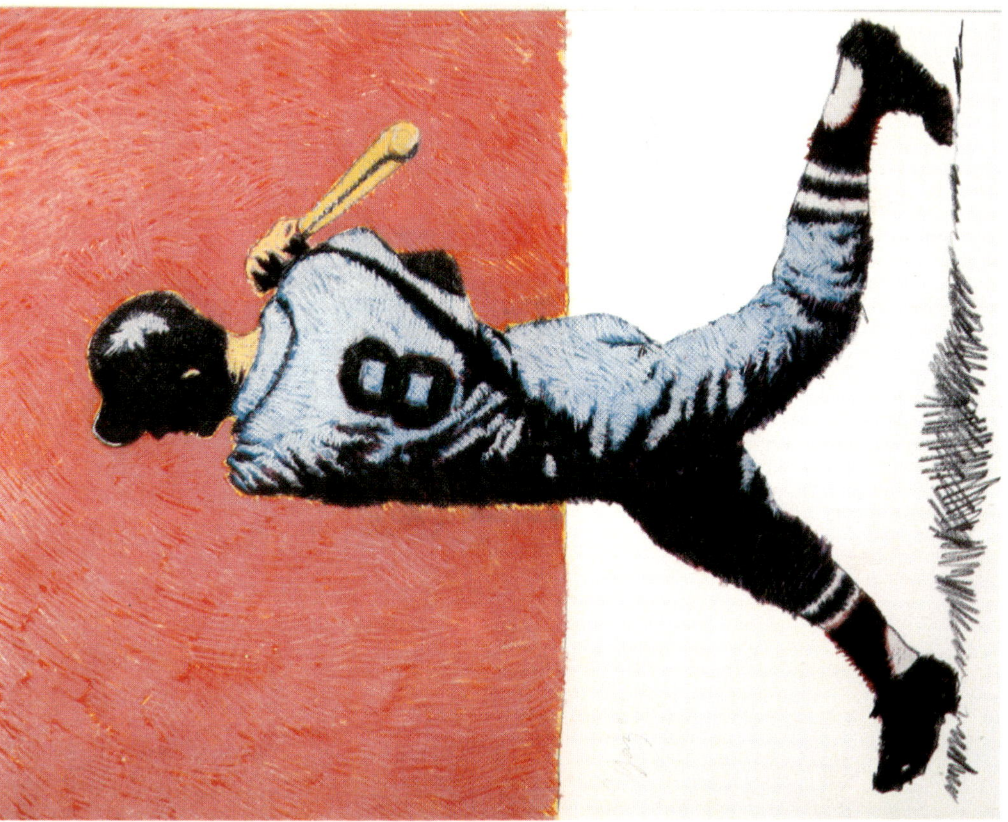

THOM ROSS
Yaz (1989)
Oil pastel on paper, 38″ x 32″
COURTESY OF GALLERY 53, COOPERSTOWN, NY,
PHOTO CREDIT RON WILCOX

FAWCETT COLUMBINE • NEW YORK

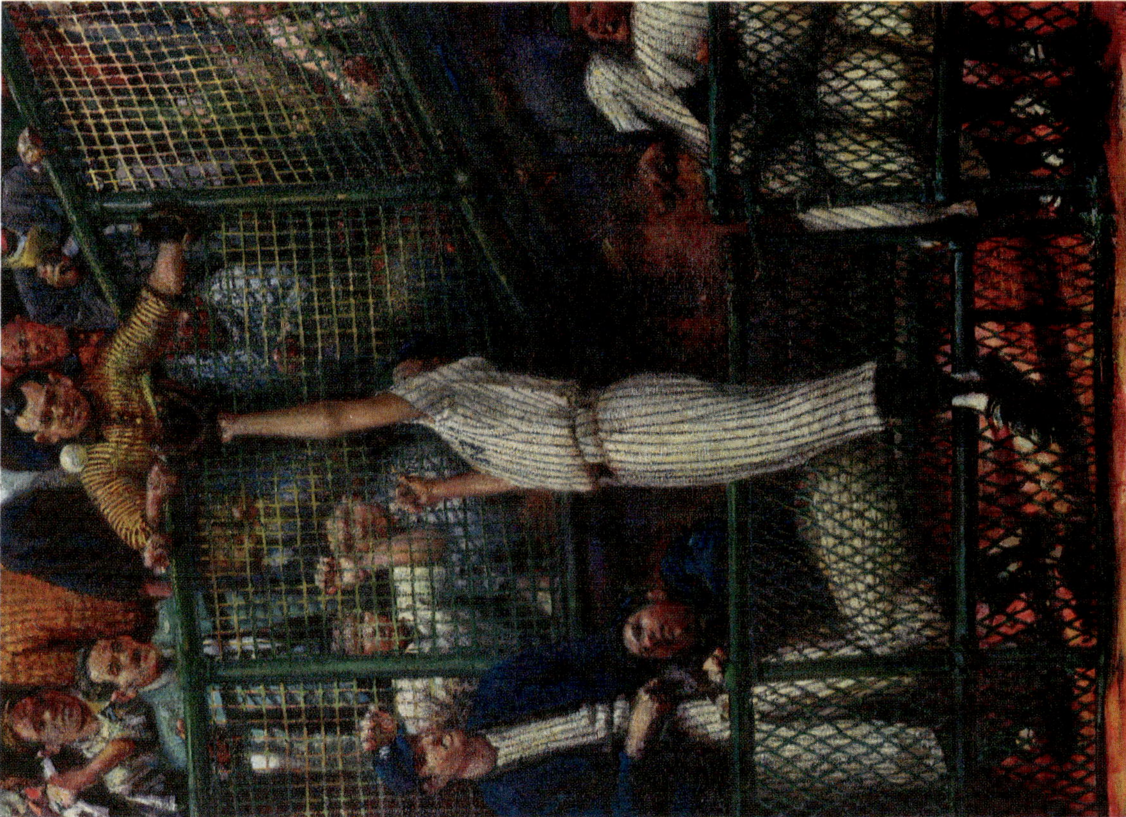

LANCE RICHBOURG
Roger Maris (1986)
Oil on canvas, 64″ x 80″
COURTESY O.K. HARRIS GALLERY, NYC

FAWCETT COLUMBINE • NEW YORK

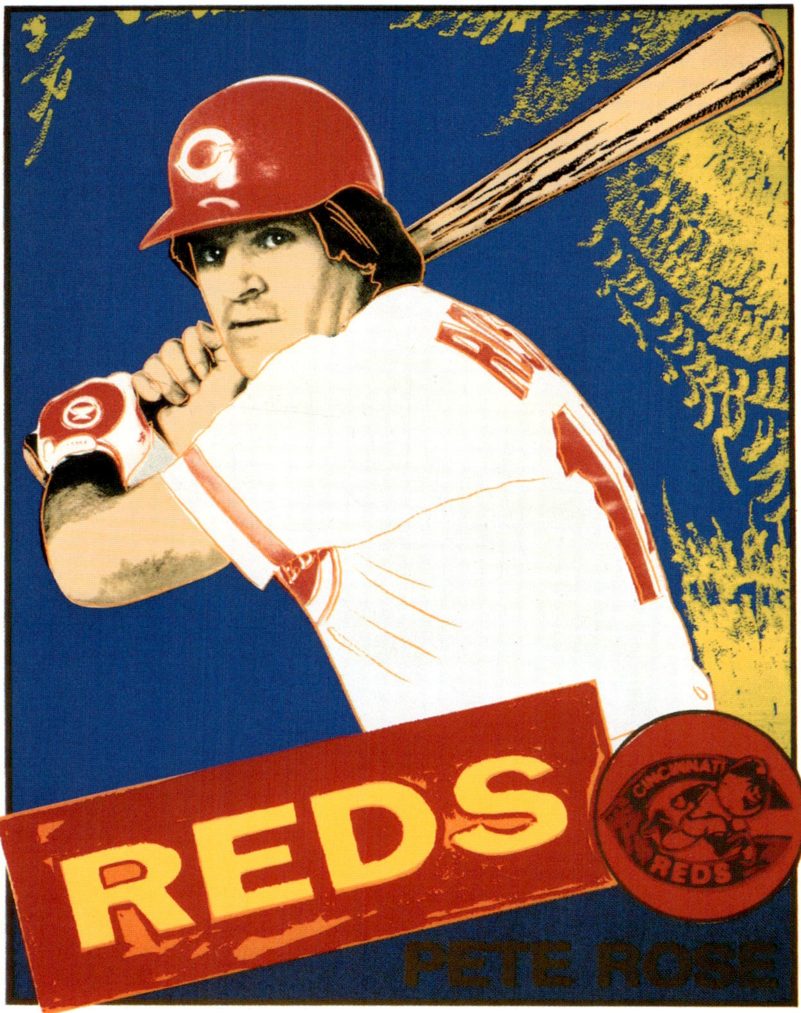
REDS
CINCINNATI
REDS
PETE ROSE

ANDY WARHOL
Pete Rose (1989)

FAWCETT COLUMBINE • NEW YORK

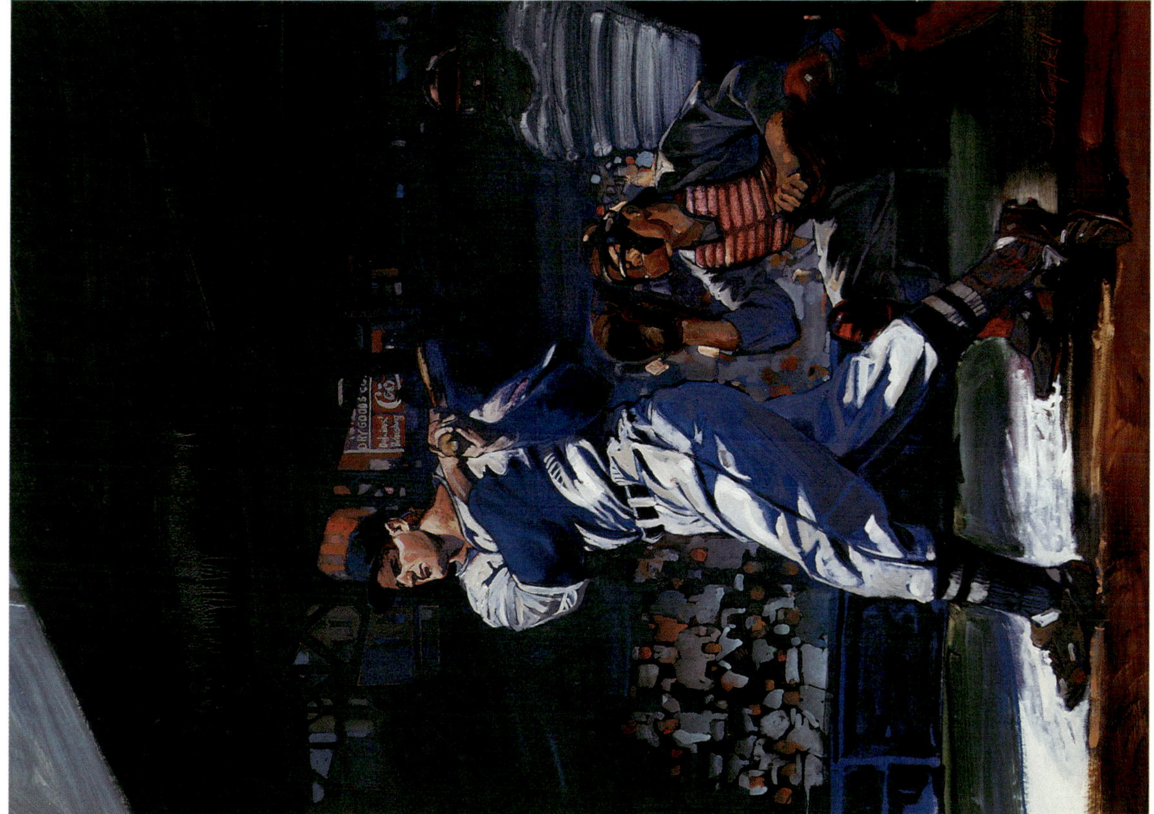

JIM CAMPBELL
Untitled (1985)
COURTESY OF MENDOLA, LTD.

FAWCETT COLUMBINE • NEW YORK

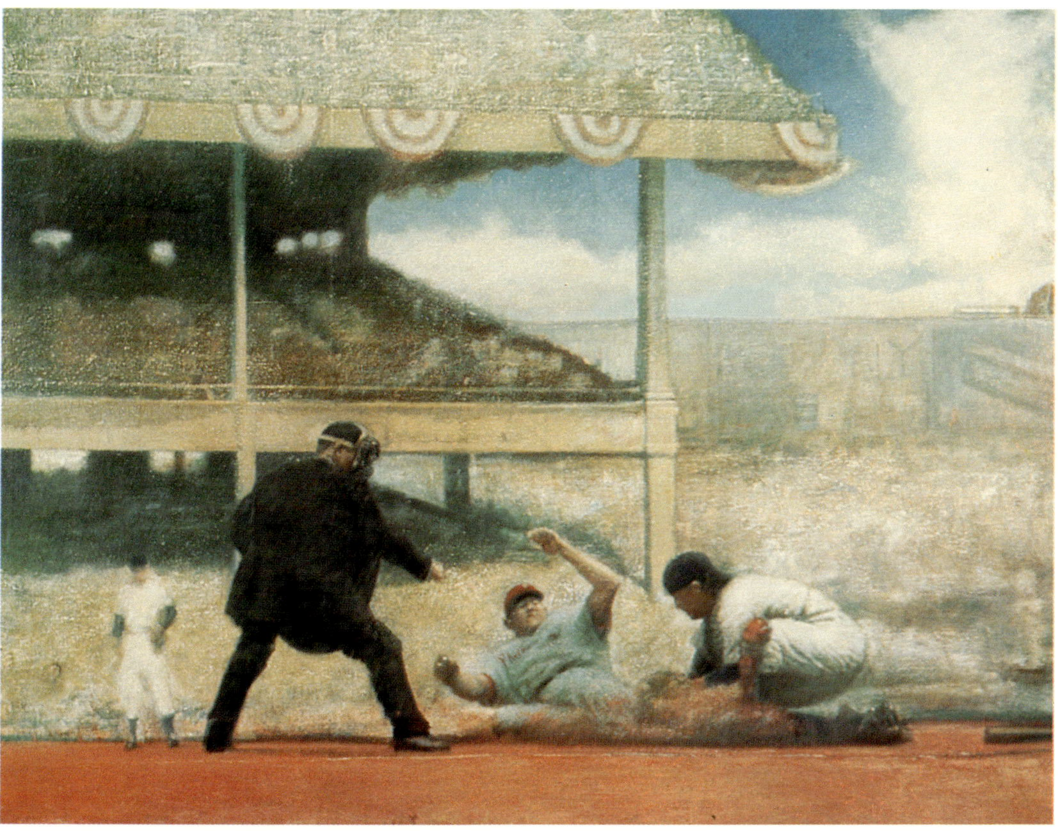

LANCE RICHBOURG
Sliding in Yankee Stadium (1979)
Oil on canvas, 66" x 77"
COURTESY O.K. HARRIS GALLERY, NYC

FAWCETT COLUMBINE • NEW YORK

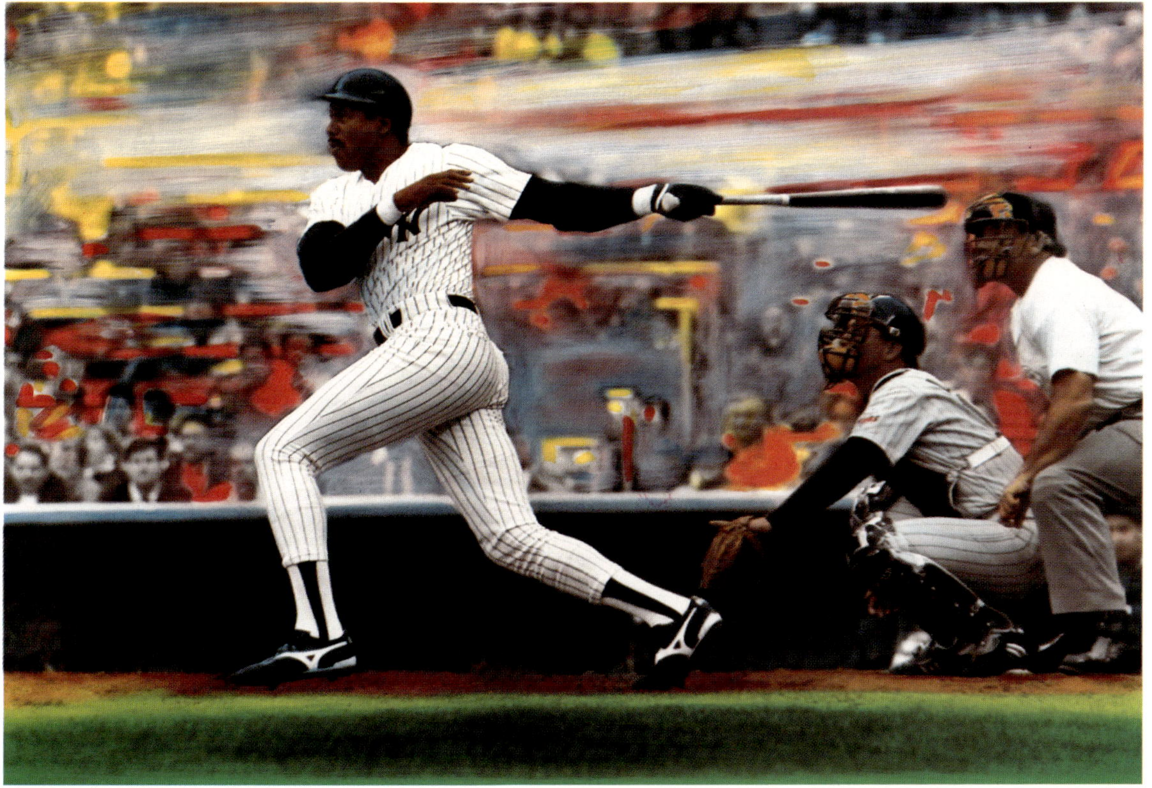

JEFFREY RUBIN
Dave Winfield (1988)
Oil on b&w photo, 41″ x 56″

FAWCETT COLUMBINE • NEW YORK

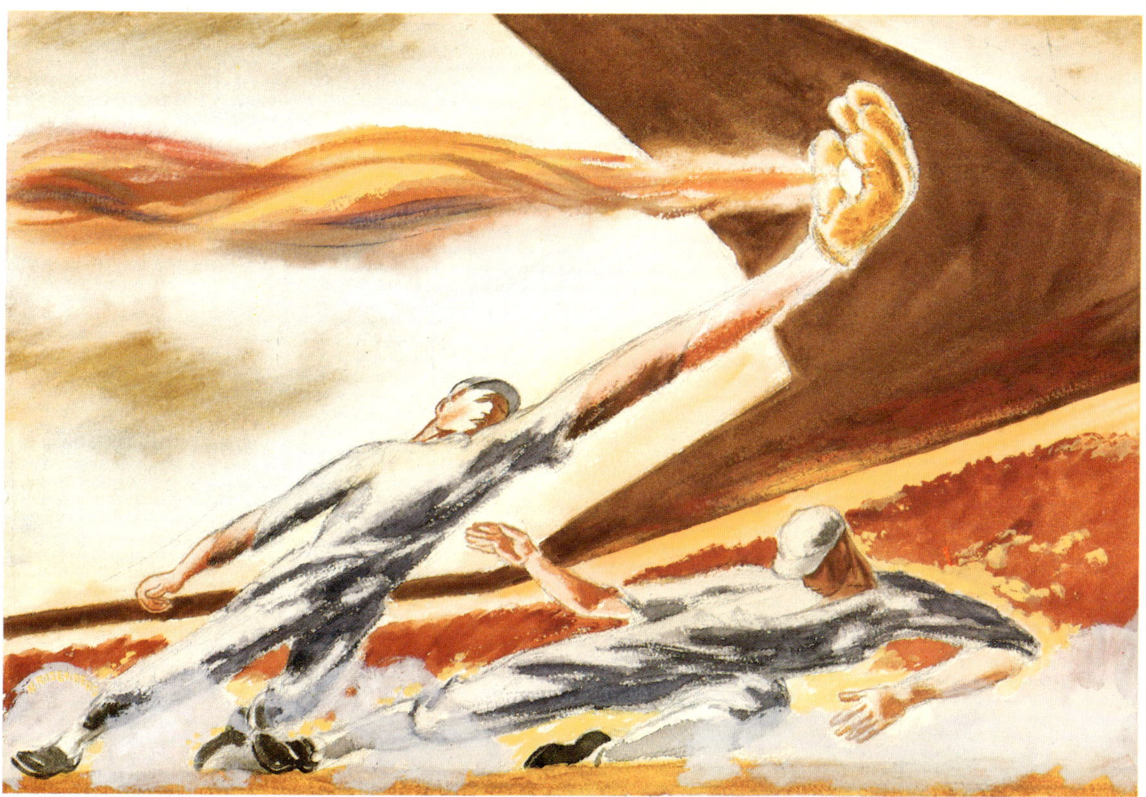

NELSON ROSENBERG (b. 1908)
Out at Third (undated)
THE PHILLIPS COLLECTION, WASHINGTON, D.C.

FAWCETT COLUMBINE • NEW YORK

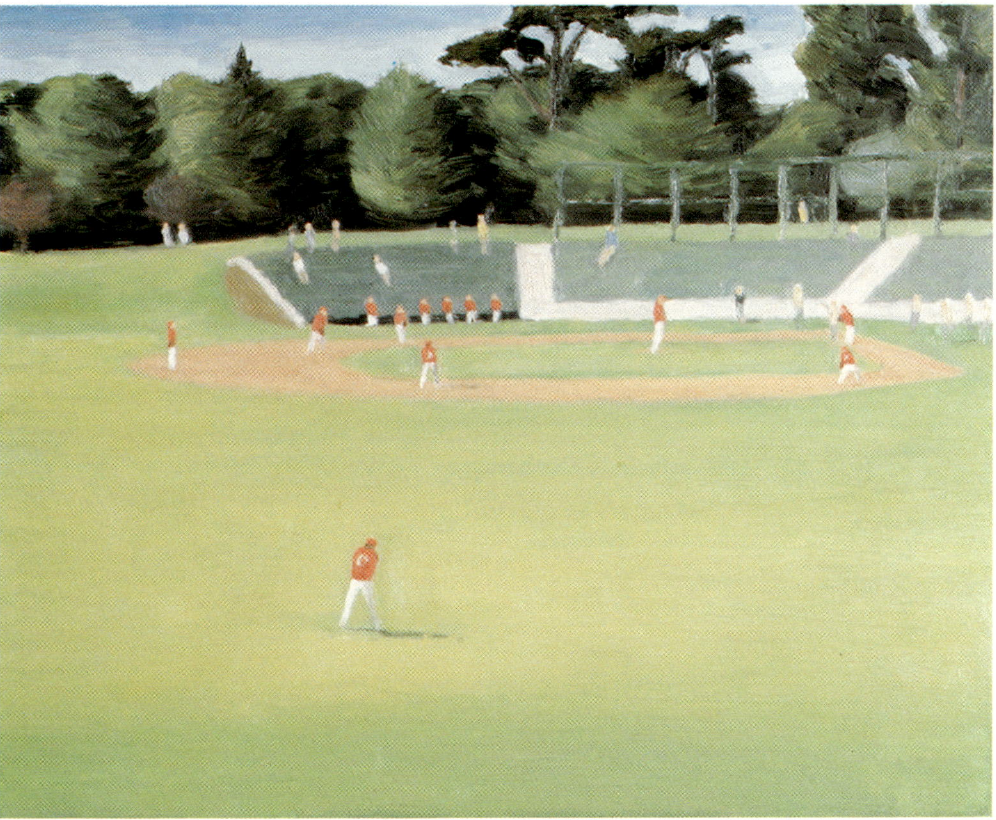

ANDREW RADCLIFFE
The Baseball Game, Golden Gate Park (1986)
Oil on canvas, 18″ x 22″
NANCY HOFFMAN GALLERY

FAWCETT COLUMBINE • NEW YORK